GULLIBLE'S TROUBLES

Written and illustrated by
Margaret Shannon

Houghton Mifflin Company

Boston

For my brother Kia
—M.S.

Many big thanks to
Kai, Matthew, Stephen B., Tim, Matthias, and Kate
for their help with this book.

www.hmco.com/trade

Library of Congress Cataloging-in-Publication Data
Gullible's troubles / written and illustrated by Margaret Shannon.
p. cm.
Summary: Although Gullible Guineapig believes everything his aunt, uncle,
and cousin tell him, they dismiss his warning about what is in the basement.
RNF ISBN 0-395-83933-5   PAP ISBN 0-618-07033-8
[1. Guinea pigs — Fiction. 2. Monsters — Fiction.] I. Title.
PZ7.S52884GU 1998
[E] — dc21 97-9567 CIP AC
Manufactured in the United States of America
WOZ 10 9 8 7 6 5 4 3

GULLIBLE GUINEAPIG was visiting Aunt Sarah,
Uncle Bernard, and Cousin Lila, all by himself.

His aunt and uncle and cousin knew Gullible would
believe anything that he was told.

"You know there are monsters all over this house,
Gullible, and in the garden too," said Cousin Lila.

"Little guinea pigs are their *favorite* thing to eat."

Gullible didn't like this idea one bit. He went to see if
Aunt Sarah needed any help. She was baking a cake.

But, although Gullible tried very hard,
he wasn't much help at all.

So Aunt Sarah said, "Did you know, Gullible, that if you eat fifty carrots one after the other, you become invisible?"

Gullible thought that sounded like great fun. Aunt Sarah gave him a big basket of carrots that were getting moldy and told him to go and eat them in the front room.

Gullible ate . . .

and ate . . .

and ate

until he'd eaten all fifty carrots. Then, feeling rather ill,
he went and looked in the mirror to see if he was invisible.

But he wasn't. He'd just gone a bit orange in the face.
"They must've been too old," Gullible said to himself,
and thought he'd go and see what Cousin Lila was doing.

Cousin Lila was dressing up for a party.

Gullible decided to dress up too,

but he started getting a bit carried away . . .

So Cousin Lila said, "Gullible, would you like to take these soccer boots of mine and try them out? They're the sort the real soccer players use."

Gullible had always wanted proper soccer boots. He got out his soccer ball, and went downstairs to put the boots on.

But they were a bit big for him, and they wobbled
when he tried to dribble the ball. Gullible decided he'd
just get used to walking in them for now and went to see
what Uncle Bernard was doing.

Uncle Bernard was very busy, so Gullible thought he would help by tidying up his papers for him.

Uncle Bernard said, "If you really want to help, Gullible, you could wash these dirty pieces of coal for me, so I can light the fire."

Gullible felt very useful as he carried the coal into the
pantry and started scrubbing it with a scrubbing brush.

But the coal never seemed
to get any cleaner,

it just got smaller and smaller

until there wasn't any left.

Gullible hurried off to find out where he could get
some more coal.

He asked Cousin Lila, who was in the front room
checking out her party dress.

"Well, the coal's in the cellar, where the cellar monster
lives," she said. "But if you walk on your hands, it won't
eat you."

The cellar was very dark.

Gullible carefully walked on his hands, down the stairs
and over to the coal chute. He could just see the cellar
monster's feet sticking out from the darkest corner.

He filled the coal bucket and made his way back up the stairs as quickly as he could, nearly bumping into his aunt at the top.

"Aunt Sarah, remember to walk on your hands, or you'll get eaten!!" Gullible cried. Aunt Sarah just laughed.

Gullible waited and waited, but Aunt Sarah didn't come back.

He ran to tell Uncle Bernard and Cousin Lila what had happened.

"What nonsense, Gullible!" said Uncle Bernard. "Lila and I will go down and find out what's going on."

Uncle Bernard and Cousin Lila didn't come back
either. But there was something coming up the cellar
stairs, something with very large, heavy feet. Gullible
thought that this would be a good time to go, but there
were those monsters in the garden to get past.

So he ran into the kitchen, quickly ate fifty nonmoldy carrots . . .

found his soccer ball and put on his new soccer boots . . .

Hey, Gullible, come back! We were just kidding.
Yes, silly, of course there aren't any monsters in the cellar . . . .
BG

and ran home.